Remarkable Ramsey, the Talking Dog

by BARBARA RINKOFF

Illustrated by LEONARD SHORTALL

SCHOLASTIC BOOK SERVICES

NEW YORK • LONDON • RICHMOND HILL, ONTARIO

Copyright © 1965 by Barbara Rinkoff. Copyright © 1966 by Scholastic Magazines, Inc. This edition is published by Scholastic Book Services, a division of Scholastic Magazines, Inc., by arrangement with William Morrow & Company, Inc.

British Commonwealth Edition..June 1967

Printed in the U.S.A.

To my children

JUNE, RICHARD, and BOB

This book belongs

To

Karen

Julie

Hickman,

1, Arden Lodge RD,

Brooklands,

Manchester 23.

Contents

1

The Surprise Gift

CHARLIE SAT AT HIS DESK, staring moodily at the blackboard. As if he cared about any silly arithmetic problems! He had problems far more important than those the teacher had put on the board.

Charlie Rich didn't want to go home after school. Any other boy in the same situation would especially want to go home on a day like this. But Charlie wasn't like anyone else. And he didn't want to go home.

The classroom pencils scratched; shoes scuffled under desks; on the wall the clock ticked. Then suddenly the last bell of the afternoon ripped through all the other noises. And Charlie had hardly started his arithmetic. Miss Wright, the teacher, called for all papers to be handed in. Charlie passed his forward with the others.

"Charles." It was the teacher speaking. "You are to stay after class and finish your problems."

Charlie stifled a grin. Fine, he thought. Now he wouldn't have to go home.

But in a moment he realized it wasn't so fine after all. The other boys in the fourth grade were looking at Charlie and whispering to each other. Charlie felt his face getting redder and redder and his mouth getting drier and drier, the way they always did when people paid a lot of attention to him.

Now one of the boys was at the teacher's desk and whispering to her. She frowned and shook her head. Then she looked at the wall clock and slowly nodded. "Charles," she said, "Frank tells me you have a special reason for going home today."

Charlie lowered his eyes and didn't say anything.

"Well," Miss Wright said, "I'll keep you for only fifteen minutes after class today, and you do as much as you can. If you haven't completed your paper, you may do it Monday, during morning recess."

A sigh rippled through the air, and the children gathered their books and filed out of the room, leaving Charlie slumped over his unfinished paper. He worked steadily until Miss Wright dismissed him. Then he made his way out into the street. He was hurrying home when he heard his name called. "Char-lie. Wait up, Charlie."

He stopped, looking back down the road. Not a person in sight. Everyone else must be gone by now, Charlie thought, and began to run.

"Char-lie."

Charlie slowed his pace and looked from left to right. He listened hard.

"Wait up." The voice was very close now.

Charlie stopped dead in his tracks, then whirled around quickly, trying to spot the speaker.

"I'm talking. Down here. *Me*."

Charlie looked down sharply. There was no one there, no one except a not-too-big, not-too-small dog. And that was hardly a someone. The animal's thin, pointy tail stood straight up, twitching rapidly back and forth as if it were a clock pendulum. Charlie stooped down and peered closely at him. The dog's dark eyes snapped merrily, and his ears stood as straight as soldiers at attention. He had an oddly shaped white crest marking his forehead, and golden-

tan short, rough hair. The dog's sides heaved, and his red tongue hung like a long ribbon out of a smiling mouth.

"Yes, me. Surprised?" the dog said plainly.

Charlie looked at him unbelievingly.

"I talk." The dog spoke even more clearly now that he wasn't panting so hard. "Lots of people don't hear me," he continued, "but if we're going to be friends, you'll have to accept it. I talk!"

Charlie swallowed hard. He opened his mouth, but no sound came out.

"You'll get used to it. We'll get along fine. You're my kind of boy." The dog's tail waved confidently, and his eyes seemed to look right through Charlie.

"I am?" Charlie managed to squeeze the words out faintly.

"Let's go, or you'll be late. The party, remember? That's why I'm speaking to you today. I'm giving you a birthday present."

"You are?"

"Sure am." The dog waved his tail pompously.

Charlie wondered how the dog knew it was his birthday. But he was even more curious about the present a mongrel dog like this could possibly give him. An old bone? A chewed-up rubber ball? A tasty torn slipper?

"Know what it is?"

Charlie shook his head.

"You'll never guess." The dog's dark eyes sparkled. "I'll have to tell. It's me!"

"*You!*"

"Every boy should have a dog. You don't have one. I've been watching you. Think we need each other, you and I."

"We do?"

"Definitely. You don't have a best friend, do you?"

Charlie looked at his shoes. "No," he said. As a matter of fact, he didn't have any real friends at all.

"Didn't think so," the dog said. "Kind of scared of most people, aren't you?"

Charlie didn't much like the word "scared." "I wouldn't say that," he protested.

"How about storekeepers? You like to talk to them?"

Charlie put his hands into his pockets and looked down. He hated to ask the price of anything.

"Strangers?" the dog continued. "Teachers? Kids —lots of them at a time? Didn't even want a party. Your mother insisted and invited all the boys in your class."

Charlie didn't have a chance to answer any of the questions.

"Thought so," the dog concluded. "Well, you can talk to me. From now on. And I'm going to talk to you." The dog trotted ahead, lifting his paws gracefully and occasionally looking back at Charlie, who followed obediently as if he were in a trance. The dog acted as if he didn't expect Charlie's mother or father to object — as if he could walk right into Charlie's house and make himself at home.

By the time Charlie reached home, his guests were waiting impatiently in the yard, where the party table was set up. He hustled into the house, and the dog followed. As soon as the door slammed, Charlie's mother's voice called from the kitchen. "Hurry, Charlie. Wash up and go out to the party as quickly as you can. They've been waiting for you. Of all days to be late!"

She hadn't seen the dog yet. Charlie took the steps two at a time, the dog bounding at his heels. He washed and then went immediately to his room to straighten up for the party.

The dog sniffed around the room, inspecting the furniture and Charlie's games and books. "Nice house. Expected it. Plenty of space in this room. I'll bed down near the window. Like to have the sun warm my back." He stood quietly for a moment, extending his legs and stretching his back, making his wiry muscles ripple.

The dog didn't seem to mind that Charlie wasn't very talkative. He was mouthing a baseball he'd found under a chair, and after a small game by himself he tossed it neatly into Charlie's toybox. "Don't want your mother thinking *I* messed up the room," he explained. "Slick down that hair. Have to look good on your birthday." He pawed his whiskers and then gave himself a shake.

Charlie smoothed down his cowlick and began fussing with his shirt collar. The dog nosed his leg gently. "Looks fine. Let's go. We're late enough already."

Charlie hung back, starting to retie his shoes.

The dog seized Charlie's pants in his mouth and pulled. "Hurry, the ice cream will melt. I prefer chocolate ice cream. Don't let them give me vanilla," he said briskly, guiding Charlie down the stairs.

Charlie moved slowly, nodding solemnly at the dog's request. Down the stairs they went and out into the yard, the dog trotting closely behind. The bright sun made Charlie blink. Then a sea of faces rose before him, and he stopped dead in his tracks. There were a lot of kids. His mother hadn't left anyone out. Like a big wave they moved forward. Frank, Tom, Mike, Jimmy, Arthur, Don, and all the rest from class. Charlie stepped backward as they rushed toward him. He was about to back up farther when his leg bumped against something firm and warm.

"Going the wrong way," the dog muttered, nosing Charlie's leg.

"Hi, Charlie," Frank called.

"About time you showed up for your own party," Mike said.

Charlie flushed and looked at his shoes. Jimmy slapped him on the back. "Let's eat," he shouted. Charlie stumbled forward, not daring to look up at the group, and the boys crowded around him, pushing him to the table.

"New dog?" Don asked, noticing the pup who was bounding about in the crowd, his tail slapping everyone's legs.

"Some mutt," Mike chimed in before Charlie could answer. "Why didn't you get a thoroughbred while you were at it?"

Charlie felt hot all over. He wished he could disappear. He glanced quickly at the dog, whose short hairs stood bristling on his back. "You don't look like a thoroughbred yourself," the dog growled. "Some manners. I've met politer alley cats."

Charlie had to smile in spite of himself. No one else seemed to hear the dog speaking. When the boys were settled in their seats around the table, Charlie's mother brought out a lighted birthday cake and placed it before him. Charlie could feel all eyes upon him. He felt a hot blush starting at the top of his body, but down at his feet there was a warm furry lump. He closed his eyes, blew out the candles, and wished hard. "Let me keep the dog. Please let me keep the dog," he repeated silently.

Everyone sang "Happy Birthday," and Charlie heard the dog's voice singing loud, clear, and off-pitch all through the song. Mrs. Rich threw the dog a bit of cake and asked whose he was. Charlie nearly choked on his own cake, but fortunately the party noise drowned out her question and she forgot it.

When his mother began to dish out the ice cream, a wet nose brushed Charlie's leg. "Chocolate, remember?" the dog whispered.

Charlie patted his rough head and glanced at the guests. No one seemed to notice anything unusual. "I'll have two chocolates," Charlie said shyly.

His mother raised her eyebrows, and everyone else laughed and kidded him about his appetite.

"I'm only having one. Honestly — the other is for the dog. He prefers chocolate."

"How do *you* know?" Don shouted.

"He tell you?" Mike screamed with laughter.

"Yes, as a matter of fact, he did," Charlie answered softly, setting the plate down in front of the dog. His face turned a brick red, because the laughter doubled as soon as he answered.

The dog looked up from his dish, his chin whiskers coated brown. His tail flicked in annoyance. "Fools!" he muttered into his ice cream.

As soon as the food was gone, the boys left the table. The dog followed, licking his chops, prancing in and out among the guests. Everyone was yelling at once, suggesting games. "Hide and Seek . . . Red Rover . . . Relay Races," they called.

"Let Charlie pick for a change — it's his birthday," Frank shouted above the rest.

Charlie flushed. Usually his schoolmates didn't ask his opinion about anything, let alone give him the choice of deciding the game. He wasn't good at games.

The dog sidled up to Charlie. "Choose Hide and Seek. I'll help you," he whispered.

Charlie hesitated, looked at the dog, and then called out, "Hide and Seek. I'll be It." Charlie shut his eyes, began to count, and everyone scrambled to hide.

". . . ninety-nine, one hundred! Here I come, ready or not!" Charlie opened his eyes and looked about the yard. Nothing moved; no one was visible. He'd never catch anyone. He'd probably be It all afternoon. Then he heard the dog chuckle.

"Let's confuse them. I'll stay here. Can't have them say I helped. I'll tell you where to look."

Charlie felt a little easier. "Okay," he said, beginning to smile.

"There, behind the garbage can. Mike. You go. I'll watch the base."

Cautiously, Charlie tiptoed over to the garbage can. "Tap, tap, Mike," he yelled, and sprinted back to the base as fast as he could go, touching it first.

Mike came dashing in and threw himself on the ground next to the dog, poking at him and pulling his ears.

The dog's ears flattened and the hair on his back bristled. "Enough of that," he growled. "Charlie, call off your friend."

"He says to leave him alone," Charlie said.

"What d'you mean, *he* says?" Mike demanded.

Charlie's face got red. He looked over at the dog, who muttered, "Forget it, Charlie. He won't understand."

They played and played, and Charlie caught everyone. Over and over he offered to be It. It was the first time he had ever enjoyed Hide and Seek.

"You sure are lucky on your birthday. You were never much good at this game before. Funny . . ."

Mike scratched his head and looked at Charlie suspiciously.

The boys tired of Charlie's success, and Frank came to the rescue by suggesting a race. They all lined up across the yard. Slowly Charlie took his place at one end of the line. He kicked at the grass and didn't even bother to look across at the finish line. He knew he'd be the last one in. He always was.

"Let's win," the dog snapped, jumping and frisking at Charlie's heels.

Charlie shook his head. "I'll never make it," he sighed.

The dog's tail whacked Charlie's leg. "If that's the way you act . . . won't even try . . . guess I'd better leave now. You'll be no fun to play with," the dog muttered, and bounded away across the yard in the direction of the finish line.

"On your mark . . . get ready . . . get set . . . *go!*" shouted Frank, and the line broke as the boys dashed off.

Charlie ran too, his eyes on the dog. He just couldn't leave. No, no, *no*, Charlie thought, and he was surprised to feel himself running as he had never run before. His legs seemed to go like wheels, carry-him swiftly across the yard. He was passing the other boys. But the dog was still far ahead. Charlie put on an extra burst of speed. Every muscle in his body was working.

"You passed the finish line. Hey, Charlie, you won," he heard the boys calling after him, but he raced on. The dog was still getting away. Charlie began to pant, his legs felt the sudden unaccustomed strain, his throat was tight. Then suddenly the dog was within reach. A moment later Charlie fell upon him.

"Stay. Stay with me," he panted.

The dog's tail beat a cooling breeze. "I think I will," he whispered. "I think I will."

By then the boys had joined Charlie. "Sure is strange," Mike kept saying to him. "Must be the birthday. Never saw you so good at everything."

The dog laughed.

"Sh," Charlie whispered, ruffling his coat and patting him on the head.

They played Red Rover and catch, and Charlie was surprised when his mother announced that it was time for everyone to leave. After the last guest had gone, Mrs. Rich began cleaning up the yard. "Oh dear, what's that dog still doing here?" she sighed. "Go home, pup. Go on now, shoo!" She threw a scrap of cake across the yard away from the house.

"Shoo — humph. Better tell her, Charlie," the dog said with annoyance.

Charlie shrugged. "How?"

"What do you mean, *how*?" his mother asked, looking at him oddly. "Don't act silly. Help me clean up. Do shoo that dog off," she added.

Charlie shook his head and looked timidly at his mother. "The dog is mine," he whispered.

His mother went on cleaning the table.

"Speak up, Charlie. She didn't hear," the dog urged.

Charlie cleared his throat and began again. "It's

my dog," he said loudly.

Charlie's mother whirled around, holding a stack of dirty plates in mid-air. "*Your* dog? Where did you get him?"

Charlie shifted his weight from one foot to the other. "He's a birthday present." He didn't dare mention who the present was from.

"Well, that's an odd gift. Children these days ask no questions. Whatever made anyone think you wanted a dog?"

"I do. I really do. Please, may I keep him?"

The dog nosed Charlie's leg. "Speak up, boy. Stand firm."

"I'm *going* to keep him." His words spilled out. "He's my birthday present. You can take all the others, but I won't let you take him. He's mine!" Charlie's fists were clenched and his face was crimson.

"I've never heard you speak up so boldly, Charlie. I'm glad to hear that you care about something so much. Perhaps a dog would be a good birthday gift."

"It will, it will," Charlie shouted. "Did you hear that? I can keep you!" Charlie stooped down and buried his face in the dog's hair.

"Now Charlie, we'll have to hear what Dad says

about this," his mother reminded him.

"He'll say yes. He's got to," Charlie said firmly.

The dog licked Charlie's face. "Stick to your guns," he murmured.

When he came home, Charlie's father examined the dog carefully. "Not much to look at," he said. "In poor shape."

"Look who's talking," snapped the dog.

"Sh," Charlie whispered.

His father inspected the dog's hair. "At least he doesn't have any fleas," he commented.

"You've got dandruff," the dog grumbled, shaking himself.

"Something strange about this animal," Mr. Rich remarked. Then looking at Charlie's anxious face, he said, "I guess he'll be all right. Feed him up a bit."

"Whoopee!" Charlie shouted.

"Let's eat," the dog added.

2

A Dignified Name

CHARLIE DASHED UPSTAIRS AFTER SUPPER, the dog following more slowly at his heels. "Come on. Let's go to my room, where we can talk," Charlie said.

"You mean *our* room," the dog reminded him.

Charlie smiled and nodded. In the bedroom he settled down in his chair. The dog yawned noisily and stretched out on the rug under the window. "If we're going to be roommates, you'd better tell me your name," Charlie said. "What is it?"

The dog rolled over on his side. "It's open," he said thoughtfully.

"What do you mean, it's open?"

"Anything you like. Choice is yours. 'Course I have the final okay."

"You mean you don't have a name?"

"Wouldn't say that exactly. I've been called lots of things. Rex, Brownie, Pal, Mutt. Tell the truth, I never had one I really liked. No class to any of them."

"What kind of name would you like?" Charlie asked.

"I've thought about it many times. It should be dignified, stately. Suited to my personality."

Charlie stared at him. He hardly looked dignified or stately.

"Look rather sedate, don't I?" The dog stretched his neck and pointed his tail stiffly. "I'm not really, though. Enjoy a good joke, and have a flexible viewpoint."

Charlie nodded. He wasn't sure what "flexible viewpoint" meant, but he already knew the dog enjoyed a joke. "How about King?" he suggested. "It's dignified."

"Commonplace."

"Scout?"

"Not stately."

Charlie bit his lip, concentrating hard. "Chief?" His face lighted up as he offered it.

"Sounds like an Indian," grumbled the dog.

Charlie sighed. He had never thought picking a name for a dog would be so difficult. "What about Champion? Star? Ranger?" The dog shook his head at each one. "Sam? Matthew Marshall? Hardy?" The dog was unimpressed.

Charlie went on, speaking half aloud. "My father knew a professor by the name of Ramsey, who was very dignified."

The dog's ears shot up. "Ramsey. That has a ring to it. Impressive. Stately."

Charlie repeated it a few times. "Ramsey. Ramsey.

You're right. It sounds good."

"Has the right flavour." The dog nodded, and his tail thumped on the floor, sounding like a muffled drumbeat. Then he got up and stood in front of Charlie. "Clever. Best name I ever had."

Charlie flushed scarlet and lowered his eyes.

"Be proud, boy, be proud. Chin up, eyes straight. Take credit gracefully."

Charlie raised his head, took a deep breath, and looked the dog square in the eye.

"Now, name me officially," the dog requested.

"How?"

"Use your imagination, boy. You've got it — use it."

Charlie thought a moment and then asked the dog to sit. He placed his hand on the dog's rough head. "I, Charles, do name you to be known from hereafter on and forever as Ramsey." The dog sat perfectly still, his ears up, his tail quiet. Charlie tapped him on the right shoulder and then on the left. "Rise, Ramsey, and go forth," he said solemnly.

The dog stood up on his hind legs and licked Charlie first on one cheek, then on the other. "Excellent ceremony. Every element of grandeur. Charlie, you're a thinking boy." Ramsey walked grandly

about the room, tail held high.

Charlie felt himself blushing at the dog's praise, but he grinned. Ramsey wasn't much to look at really, but he certainly acted as if he were something very special. Charlie wished he could give him something to mark the occasion. A collar, he decided — a dog needed a collar. And that reminded Charlie of something else.

Ramsey eyed him with concern. "Feel okay? You look disturbed."

"Great," Charlie said quickly. "I was just thinking, I'll have to get you a license."

"Humph." Ramsey tossed his head. "Seems nutty to me. People run around loose without a license. Can't figure why we dogs need them. Dogs certainly get into less trouble than people."

"I know. I'm sorry. That's the way it has to be," Charlie said. "But don't worry, I'll get you the best-looking collar you ever saw," he added eagerly.

"Collar!" Ramsey exploded. "Never wear one. Cuts my neck."

"But . . . but I'm afraid you'll have to."

"Who says?"

"The law. Please, Ramsey, I don't want them to take you away. Please wear a collar."

The dog growled low in his throat and flattened his ears. His tail twitched rapidly. "Can't see it. Don't want to." Then seeing Charlie's worried face, he added softly, "All right. Just for you."

Charlie smiled. "I'll get you a beaut. The handsomest collar ever made. We'll get it tomorrow. We'll pick it out together."

3

Almost in Trouble

AT BREAKFAST, Charlie announced his plans. "I'm getting Ramsey his license and collar this morning."

"Sorry dear, today's Saturday and I'm busy. I can't take you," his mother answered. "I've only a week till the school fair, you know."

"But we planned to go this morning," Charlie insisted.

"Don't be unreasonable, Charles. There's no rush. Ramsey can wait a day or two."

Charlie's father came into the kitchen and sat down at the table. "Who's Ramsey?" he asked.

"He is," Charlie said, pointing to the dog.

"That's a fancy name for a mongrel," Mr. Rich observed.

"Please, Crandall!" Charlie's mother sighed.

"Look who's talking about names," Ramsey muttered. His tail flicked back and forth rapidly.

"Charlie wants to go to town to get the dog's license and collar this morning, and I can't possibly go with him," said Mrs. Rich.

"Well, don't count on me. I've got a million chores to attend to this week end," Charlie's father said quickly.

"But Dad —"

"No buts, Son. The answer is no."

Charlie lowered his eyes and pouted.

"Who needs them?" Ramsey said. "You have feet. I have feet. Let's walk."

Charlie hesitated. He didn't like to go on errands by himself. He hated to go into a store and have to tell the salesman what he wanted. And getting a dog license meant going to the Post Office. Charlie shook his head and frowned.

"Come on. Nothing to it," the dog argued.

"But —"

"No buts, Charlie. They won't mind. You'll see. Try it." Ramsey pawed the ground impatiently.

Charlie raised his head and looked squarely at his parents. "We can go alone. It's not so far. We can manage."

"Well!" Charlie's mother looked startled.

"That so?" His father eyed him strangely. "I thought you were the one who refused to go anywhere alone. Glad to see the day!"

Charlie looked at his mother. She smiled broadly at him. "Be home in time for lunch, Son. Watch the crossings, and pick a nice collar for Ramsey."

"*I'll* do the picking," the dog said.

Charlie grinned, got some money from his father, and left the house in a hurry, Ramsey running alongside him. The sun sparkled overhead, and a whitish glare rose from the pavement. Charlie walked quickly. The dog sprinted silently at his side. The Post Office wasn't very far, and Charlie and Ramsey reached it in record time. Charlie sat down on the broad front steps of the building.

"This it?" said the dog. "Let's go in."

"Wait." Charlie's voice sounded hesitating. "What will I say?"

"One dog license, please."

"Yes, but suppose they ask questions?" Charlie was beginning to feel sorry he'd come alone.

"Answer," Ramsey said firmly, getting up and nosing the screen door open.

Charlie jumped up in alarm. He was afraid Ramsey would be sent to the dog pound if he were caught roaming around the Post Office alone, especially without a license. Charlie hurried after the dog into the building.

A tall man leaned over the desk and stared at them. "Want something?" he asked in a sharp voice.

"Mmmm." Charlie's reply was more like a hum than an answer.

The dog's nose prodded his legs. "Speak up," he ordered.

"Yes sir," Charlie practically shouted.

"What can I do for you?" the clerk asked. He frowned at Charlie, as if he were annoyed at being disturbed.

Charlie pointed to the dog. "I want a license for him," he said.

The man rummaged in his files and took out a small white printed card. He handed it to Charlie. On it was printed in bold black type:

Application for a Dog License

For a moment the words floated before Charlie's eyes. "Can you fill it out yourself?" the clerk inquired gruffly.

Charlie looked the card over. "I'm not sure," he whispered.

"Give it here. I'll fill it out. You tell me the answers."

Charlie handed back the card. The man looked sternly at him. "Dog's sex — male or female?" he asked.

"Male," Charlie answered.

"Fee . . . $2.25. That goes here," the clerk muttered, his pen scratching on the paper. He asked and answered the next few questions by himself. "Village . . . Broad Creek. County . . . McIntire." Then he looked up. "Owner's name?" he inquired.

"Charles Rich," Charlie answered proudly, leaning over the desk to watch his name written in as owner.

"Street?"

"Franklin."

"Phone number?"

"Broad Creek 6-8736."

"Dog's name?"

"Ramsey."

The man looked up sharply at Charlie and then let his gaze fall on the dog. "How do you spell that?" he asked sourly.

"Illiterate!" muttered the dog.

Charlie shivered and looked inquiringly at Ramsey.

"R-a-m-s-e-y," the dog whispered to Charlie, who spelled it out for the clerk.

"Age?" the man continued.

Ramsey bristled. "Now wait a minute! That's personal," he growled.

Charlie bit his lip. Then he murmured softly, "He won't say."

The clerk put down his pen. "If you're a smart

aleck you can leave right now, young man. I've plenty of work to do. Don't waste my time," he said in a sharp tone. Ramsey bared his teeth, and Charlie bent down quickly to quiet him before there was trouble. The clerk glared at Charlie, then looked Ramsey over from nose to tail. "I'll write in seven years old," he said. "Now, what breed is he? Mongrel terrier?"

A low laugh rumbled in the dog's throat. "Say international thoroughbred."

Charlie hesitated. If the clerk got angry again there was no telling what might happen. Maybe he'd never get the license. Then Ramsey would surely be taken to the dog pound. He stood silently.

The clerk didn't seem to notice that he didn't answer. "Colour . . . tan," he continued.

Ramsey shook his head. "Hold it. Golden tan. Tell him to write golden tan, Charlie." Charlie flushed and looked at the dog. Ramsey seemed annoyed. "Go on — tell him," he snapped.

Charlie didn't know what to do. Should he risk getting the clerk irritated again? But if he ignored the dog's request . . . He gulped and in a meek voice said, "Golden tan, sir."

The clerk gave him an annoyed look. "Markings?" he went on.

"A white crest on the forehead," Charlie answered.

"Either ear cut off, wholly or in part?"

"Nope," Charlie put in quickly before Ramsey could comment.

"Last question. Is he a seeing-eye dog, or a war dog, or anything else special?"

Charlie's mouth opened, but he stopped himself before a word got out. How could he say that Ramsey talked? The clerk would think he was crazy. He was mad enough already. Charlie didn't dare risk getting him madder. He decided not to answer. He needed to get that license for Ramsey, and he had to get this man to sell it to him.

"Well?" the man asked. He began to push the application away from him.

"Please let him give me the license," Charlie thought to himself.

The clerk stared at Charlie for a long moment, then he shrugged. "Okay, sign here," he said, shoving the license form toward Charlie.

Charlie grabbed the pen and scribbled his name on the line. He paid the fee, and clutching the license escaped outside as quickly as he could.

Ramsey walked in a stately way behind him, glancing neither to left nor right, his tail held high.

"Boy, am I glad that's over," Charlie sighed, as they walked down the street.

"Nosy, wasn't he?" Ramsey sniffed.

Charlie wiped his forehead with his hand. "I thought for a while that we might never get your license," he said.

Ramsey tossed his head. "You handled him well," he answered.

Charlie thought it over for a moment, then he stood up a little taller. "I did, didn't I?" he said. He began to smile, and they continued the short walk to the hardware store in contented silence.

4

A Narrow Escape

As THEY CROSSED THE STREET to the hardware store, Charlie remembered old Mr. Crisp, the owner. Mr. Crisp hovered over his customers, peering down his glasses, and supervised their every move. Many times he had stared hard at Charlie, as if he were daring him to touch something. Charlie's father said Mr. Crisp acted as if he didn't want anybody to buy anything.

Charlie squared his shoulders and was about to push open the screen door when something caught his eye. A small white piece of cardboard with unevenly printed black letters was propped at the bottom of the display window near the door. It said:

No Dogs Allowed — Positively!

and the "positively" was underlined. Charlie stared at it. He had never noticed the sign before. But he hadn't had a dog before either. "Now what?" Charlie thought.

Ramsey looked inquiringly at him.

Charlie fidgeted nervously. "How will we get the collar now?" he thought. The idea of going into the store alone was something he hated to consider. Finally he spoke. "The sign says you can't come in, Ramsey. Do you think I should go alone?" he asked reluctantly.

The dog snorted. "Not on your life. *I'm* picking the collar, remember?"

Charlie shook his head. "You don't know Mr. Crisp. When he says 'positively,' he means it."

"And when I say *I* pick it, I pick it." Ramsey nosed the screen door.

"Whoa! We can't walk in that way."

"I'm for storming him." The dog chuckled.

Charlie's eyebrows shot up. "We can't do that." He stood stock still, a frown on his face. After a moment he moved quickly to the corner of the building, with the dog following close on his heels. Charlie picked through a piled stack of empty cartons while Ramsey sniffed at them curiously. Charlie was making a decision. He nodded his head and leaned down to pick up a sharp stone. "There," he grunted, punching one hole and then another in the side of the carton. Then he ripped off the flaps of the box and smoothed down the edges. "There," he said again, holding out the box for inspection. "How do you like it?"

Ramsey cocked his head, looking sideways at Charlie. "Lovely," he snapped. "I give up. What is it?"

Charlie grinned. "It's your disguise, silly. If you're under the box, you can sneak through the store after me, and Mr. Crisp won't see you."

The dog's ears twitched, and he ran his tongue over his mouth as he considered the idea. Then his tail beat fast, and he began to nod. "Agreed," he said, trotting over to the box.

Charlie carefully lowered the box over Ramsey, and the dog disappeared. "Okay? Can you see?" Charlie asked.

"A-okay." The dog's voice sounded muffled and hollow.

"Let's go." Charlie walked briskly up to the door of the hardware store and pushed it open, making the doorbell tinkle. The cardboard box glided forward after him.

Charlie felt as if he had walked into a cave. The store was almost dark; it was empty and quiet, shadowy and echoing. Charlie raised up on his tiptoes. Then slowly he made his way past a display of toilet plungers standing like soldiers in a line. "Careful, Ramsey," he hissed. *Plop, plop, plop, plop.* Down went the first plunger, then the second, and the third, and the fourth.

"Well, if it isn't Charlie!" From out of nowhere Mr. Crisp sprang at him. He peered down his sharp nose and rubbed his bony hands together.

Charlie caught his breath and then stooped quickly to right the plungers. "Don't move," he whispered to Ramsey. "Don't even breathe." Then he rose slowly, finding Mr. Crisp crouched over him.

"Looking for something, Charlie?" Mr. Crisp wheezed.

Charlie gulped. "Yes sir. I want a dog collar."

"For yourself?"

"No sir, for my dog." Charlie shifted his weight and coughed.

"Hmmm." The storekeeper eyed the cardboard box. "Can't recall leaving this here," he muttered. He was about to pick up the box when the doorbell tinkled. Mr. Crisp turned and squinted toward the front of the store. "Ah, Mrs. Spencer! I'll be right with you," he called. Then he looked back at Charlie. "The dog collars are in the rear alcove. Mind you, don't touch anything else," he warned, and stomped off toward the new customer.

Charlie waited until Mr. Crisp was at the front of the store, safely out of sight. Then he made his way to a crowded little alcove at the rear of the store which was devoted to such assorted items as bins of birdseed, sacks of sheep manure and other fertilizers, rubber mice and bones, parakeet swings and mirrors, and dog collars. The box inched forward directly behind him.

Ramsey sneezed and the box shuddered. "Rich aroma," he remarked, as the side of his box bumped into a sack of sheep manure.

Charlie giggled, guiding him away from the sack. "Quick, look at these." He lifted one end of the box and pointed to the rack of collars that hung from the wall. The dog looked silently. Then he stood on his hind legs and nosed through the collars, pausing every so often to examine one more closely. Charlie sat down on a bag of manure in the doorway of the alcove, keeping an eye out for Mr. Crisp. Within moments the dog decided.

"Here we go. Unhook this one," he said briskly.

Obediently, Charlie unhooked the collar the dog held between his teeth. Ramsey held his head high, jutting his chin forward to stretch his neck for the collar. Carefully, Charlie buckled a deep purple leather collar with bright silver stars nailed into it around the dog's neck.

"Well?" Ramsey asked haughtily.

Charlie cleared his throat. "Lovely," he whispered. "You look like a head wizard or something." He wasn't sure whether he meant that as a compliment or not. The collar was certainly a weird one.

"True, true." Ramsey nodded.

"The purple is very kingly," Charlie offered.

"You're right," the dog said. "That's it."

"Are you sure? You certainly decide on things quickly. I can never make up my mind that fast."

"Positive. Hate dawdling. Make up my mind, then act. Nothing to it. Ought to learn that, Charlie. Don't procrastinate."

Charlie hadn't the vaguest idea what "procrastinate" meant, but he wasn't going to admit that to any dog, not even Ramsey. He removed the collar from the dog's neck and eased the box back over him. "While I pay for this, you sneak toward the door. I'll meet you there." He started back through the store to the counter, whistling loudly so Mr. Crisp wouldn't notice the dog.

Before he had gone more than a few steps, Mr. Crisp cut across the store toward him. "No whistling in my store," he roared. His beady eyes stared past Charlie at the box. It was moving down the aisle ever so slightly. Charlie followed Mr. Crisp's gaze and he froze in horror. Why didn't Ramsey have the sense to stand still? Why did he keep on moving as if their plans were proceeding smoothly? Charlie held his breath, hoping Mr. Crisp would think his eyes were failing or that he was seeing things. Slowly Mr. Crisp turned his gaze on Charlie. "Wasn't that box with you when you came in?" he said sharply.

Charlie was trying to think of an answer when *wham* — the box rammed into a stack of pots and pans! It stopped dead as the pots tumbled noisily, bounced on top of it, and then landed on the floor. A big round soup pot clattered down, landing on its side. Charlie stood by helplessly as it rolled across the floor straight onto Mr. Crisp's toes. With one great shove he pushed Charlie aside and stared at the heap, rocking silently on his heels.

"I'm sorry, Mr. Crisp," Charlie said softly.

The storekeeper turned and glared at him. "What's in that box?" he demanded. His eyes flicked over Charlie, then he turned and stamped down the aisle straight toward the disguised Ramsey.

Charlie wished the floor would cave in and swallow him up. Even an earthquake would do — anything to get him out of the store. Mr. Crisp was next to the box, his bony hands almost touching it. Charlie swallowed hard and leaped forward. "Don't touch that box, Mr. Crisp!" he shouted.

The storekeeper's hands stopped in mid-air. He

turned and eyed Charlie. "And why not?" he inquired.

"Because . . . because my snake's in there," Charlie blurted out.

"*Snake!*" shrieked Mr. Crisp. "You can't bring a snake into a store!"

"Why not? Your sign only says no dogs. It doesn't say anything about snakes." Charlie looked blankly up at Mr. Crisp.

The old man's hand trembled, and he backed away from the box. "G-g-get that out of here," he stuttered.

Charlie held out the dog collar. "I'll pay you for this," he said, digging down into his pocket for the money.

Mr. Crisp extended his hand to take it, but he never moved his eyes from the box. "Dogs, snakes, what next?" he muttered shaking his head.

Charlie walked down the aisle toward the box. "Let's go, Snakey," he said loudly. Charlie could hear Ramsey hiss loudly as the box slithered forward. Across the store and out the front door they went, never pausing a second until they were safely around the corner. There Charlie flipped the box off the dog. "We made it," he sighed, and he leaned down to attach the new collar around Ramsey's neck.

The dog slithered around Charlie's legs, shooting his tongue forward. "How's that for acting?" he hissed.

Charlie laughed. "Terrific," he said, trying to step out of the circle the dog was making around him.

"Not bad yourself," Ramsey returned. "Clever, thinking up that snake idea. Yes sir, quick thinking. Handled that with skill." The dog nodded and waved his tail in approval.

Charlie puffed out his chest. Then after a moment he began to giggle. "Poor old Crisp, he'll never get over it."

"He'll be busy for the rest of the day making a new sign," said the dog, chuckling.

No Dogs, Snakes, Cats, Tigers, or Crocodiles — Positively!

The noon whistle blew loudly in their ears. "Boy, we'd better get going. We'll be late for lunch," Charlie cried, starting to run.

"Not that!" Ramsey shouted, bounding ahead with a sudden burst of speed.

They raced almost all the way home and were quite breathless when they entered the house. The kitchen table was set, and Charlie's mother and father had already begun their lunch by the time Charlie and Ramsey joined them. "Made it." Charlie gasped, slipping into his seat. Ramsey didn't waste a second in attacking the bones piled in his dish on the floor.

"Well, I never!" Charlie's mother said in astonishment, looking directly at the dog's new collar.

Charlie's father choked on his coffee as he followed her gaze. "Who picked *that?*" he asked, fingering his flowery bow tie.

Looking up, Ramsey stopped gnawing on his bone. "Who picked your tie?" he muttered.

Charlie coughed. "We did," he answered. "You'd be surprised at how the stars really shine, Dad."

His father put his hand to his eyes as if he were shielding them. "Bet I wouldn't."

"Did everything go smoothly, dear? Did you get the license?" his mother interrupted.

"Yes," Charlie answered proudly. "No trouble at all."

5

Ramsey Volunteers

THE WALK TO TOWN had made Charlie hungry. He was so busy filling his plate that he only half listened to his parents' conversation. They were talking about the school fair, which was to take place at the end of next week. Charlie's mother was one of the organizers of the yearly event. Charlie remembered her worries last year. Had she ordered enough food? Would all her helpers be sure to come? At the last minute Mrs. Green, who was to sell the flowers, had gone sick. In despiration Mrs. Rich had tried to get Charlie to assist at the stall. Before he admitted that he was too shy to help out, he was saved because someone else volunteered.

His mother's voice droned on, interrupted every now and then by his father sympathizing and offering advice. One phrase filtered through to Charlie above the crunching noise he was making as he chewed a stalk of celery. ". . . maybe Charlie can help out."

His father's words made Charlie stop in the middle of a bite. He held the celery in mid-air as if it were a flag.

"Would you, Charlie?" his mother asked, thinking he had been following the conversation.

Charlie gulped. "Would I what?"

"Help with the fair. I thought this year we'd have some new features especially for the children."

Suddenly Charlie wasn't hungry any longer. With deliberate care he placed the celery on his plate and pushed it away.

"One of the older boys is bringing his horse to give rides to the children. We'd like to have some other events that children would like," his mother continued.

Charlie listened carefully. Mother hadn't said she wanted him to do anything. She was just asking for ideas. He tilted back his chair, rocking on the rear legs. "Well, you could have a shooting gallery," he

offered, thinking of something he'd always wanted
to try. His mother shook her head uncertainly.
"What about a baseball toss?"

"An exhibition of dog tricks?" Ramsey whispered.

"An exhibition of dog tricks?" Charlie repeated
automatically.

His mother's eyes widened, and she nodded. His
father nodded too. Charlie ducked his head and
smiled at Ramsey. His parents seemed very pleased
with the suggestion. "Will you do it?" his mother
asked.

Charlie looked around quickly. She was directing
the question at *him*. He squirmed. "Me?" came out
of his mouth in a tiny squeak.

"Ramsey seems fairly intelligent," his father said, glancing at the dog. "You could teach him a few tricks and then have him perform for the children."

Charlie froze in his seat. Floating before his mind's eye was a sea of faces. Sticky faces full of candy floss and jelly apples. Laughing faces and open mouths full of teeth. Crying faces of squawking babies who wanted their mothers. Charlie could see himself on a stage with a million eyes all looking at him. He opened his mouth to speak to his parents, but nothing came out. He tried again and his voice cracked. That had happened once at a school play. Everyone in the auditorium had laughed. Slowly he shook his head and slumped down into his chair.

His father smiled at him. "Don't worry, Son. I'll give you a good manual on dog training."

"We don't need a book, Charlie," Ramsey murmured. Charlie threw him a look of despair. "Say yes, Charlie. We'll do it. We'll be the hit of the fair." Ramsey's pointy tail waved furiously back and forth, and he smiled broadly.

Charlie leaned forward to stare at the dog in disbelief. He couldn't do it. All those people. Kids from school. Parents. He shivered. Oh no, he wasn't going to make a fool of himself again.

"What do you say, Charlie? Will you do it?" his mother asked.

Charlie didn't dare look up. He sat rigid in his chair, slowly moving his head back and forth.

"Come on, Charlie," Ramsey urged.

"But —" Charlie began.

"We'll be a sensation," Ramsey roared, rolling onto his back and kicking his feet in the air.

"Look at that, Charlie. There's trick number one," his father shouted.

"What do you say, dear?" his mother asked again.

Charlie watched the dog romp for a few seconds, then halfheartedly he whispered, "Okay."

The first thing that greeted Charlie's eyes the next morning was a small, worn-looking gray book lying on the chair next to his bed. Lazily he reached out for it.

"Your father honoured us with that. Tiptoed in a while ago. Left it there." Ramsey yawned noisily, running his tongue over his mouth. He got up from under the window, shook himself, and stretched one hind leg and then the other.

Charlie sat up in bed and examined the book. The title, *Dog Tricks*, appeared neatly in bold red block letters on the cover. He thumbed the pages thoughtfully.

Ramsey slowly walked to the bed, bounded up in one leap, and settled himself among the covers. His large dark eyes studied the pages as Charlie turned them. They looked at the book wordlessly. There were pictures of a dog doing each trick, and a few paragraphs explaining how to go about training a dog to perform the trick. Charlie and Ramsey were so engrossed in the text that they didn't hear Charlie's father enter the room. They were quite startled to hear his voice.

"Morning, Son," he said, beaming, and walked over to pat Ramsey's head. "I dug up that old book in the attic last night. I knew it was around somewhere. I used it to train my dog when I was a boy. It's a good book. We won a prize at a pet show by using it. Of course, that was years ago, but the methods are still the same. Dogs aren't any smarter today than they were then."

"Neither are people," Ramsey snapped. Charlie closed his hands around the dog's snout to shut him up.

"Give the book here." Mr. Rich put out his hand. "I'll point out a few tricks that you might try."

Charlie handed the book to his father. Ramsey

nestled down in the covers, one ear cocked to the conversation.

"Here we are now. Training a dog to sit isn't very difficult." Charlie's father pointed to the next. "We can do that."

"So can I," Ramsey retorted.

"Teaching him to beg will be easy. You can use a biscuit to train him. He'll like that."

"Now you're talking," said the dog, chuckling. Charlie gave Ramsey a playful poke.

"Most dogs catch fairly well," continued Mr. Rich. "You can practise throwing him a ball."

"Use a bone, Charlie. I'll try harder with a bone!" said Ramsey eagerly. Charlie grinned.

"I think you'll be able to teach the dog these tricks by yourself, Son. Of course, if you need any help, call on me. I'll start you off on one trick right now. It's a little more difficult, so I'll give you a hand. Here, Ramsey. Down, boy. Here." Charlie's father pointed to the floor in front of his feet.

The dog lifted his head and stared at him.

"Go on, Ramsey," Charlie urged, giving the dog a gentle shove.

Ramsey raised himself with deliberate care, yawned loudly, and let himself slide down the covers to the floor.

"Now we throw this," Mr. Rich said, tossing a slipper across the floor. "Then we point to the object and say *fetch!*"

Ramsey's ears twitched at the loud command. "I'm not deaf," he growled.

"Pick it up," Charlie urged.

"No Son, you must say *fetch*, or you'll confuse him," his father insisted.

Ramsey yawned. "When you've come to a decision, let me know," he said, closing his eyes wearily.

"*Fetch!*" Charlie's father raised his voice for the command.

The dog winced, and then trotted lazily over to the slipper and picked it up. With a sigh he trotted back and laid the slipper at Mr. Rich's feet.

"Good dog. Say, he's a smart one, Charlie. We'd better practise, though. This might be beginner's luck." Charlie's father gave the slipper another toss. "*Fetch,*" he bellowed.

Ramsey shook his head. "Not again!" he said firmly.

"I think I can manage, Dad," Charlie said.

"Fine, Son. If you need me, just holler." His father smiled and started out of the room. "You only have next week to practise. You'll have to work hard, but I'm sure you'll make it," he called over his shoulder.

"Humph," Ramsey snorted. "Those tricks are for fools."

Charlie stared at the dog. "You mean you won't do them?"

"Not a chance." Ramsey lifted his head haughtily.

"But I promised Mother," Charlie said in a low voice.

"What else is in that silly book?"

Charlie grabbed the book quickly and flipped through the pages. "How to Shake Hands. Play Dead Dog. Balancing an Object." Charlie looked up to see how Ramsey was reacting to these new suggestions.

The dog twitched his tail violently and seemed to be frowning. "Any more?" he growled.

Charlie looked back at the book. "Taking an Object to Another Person. Singing. Making a Bow."

Charlie glanced at the dog. He seemed to be considering thoughtfully. His head nodded, and his tail thumped a steady beat.

Suddenly Ramsey grinned. "Got it. I'll do those tricks — but my way."

Charlie nodded, but he was rather sceptical "What will you do?"

"I'll surprise you."

"If we're partners, don't you think I ought to know?"

Ramsey shook his head.

Charlie felt a cold shiver ripple down his back. How could he be sure Ramsey would know how to perform tricks before an audience? He had never really seen him do any except fetch. The thought of being in front of a big crowd was bad enough, but not knowing what to expect, or whether to expect anything at all, was too much for Charlie. "Couldn't you please show me part of our act in private?" he asked.

Ramsey flicked his tail in annoyance. "Won't take my word, eh? Have to be convinced."

Charlie was about to protest when to his relief the dog began muttering half aloud.

"Okay, okay. It's against my principles, but I'll

give you a sample." Ramsey drew himself up to his full height, tail pointing straight at the ceiling. "Get this," he said. "You're offering me a bone. I'm supposed to beg for it."

Charlie nodded and held out his hand, pretending that there was a bone in it. The dog rose on his hind legs, walked gracefully over to Charlie, and bowed. Then he pretended to snap the bone from Charlie's hand. Before Charlie could say a word, Ramsey, holding the imaginary bone between his teeth, saluted smartly with his paw and backed off.

Charlie gasped in delight.

"And if that's not enough," the dog said, warming to the occasion, "how's this for talent?" Remaining on his hind legs, his paws clasped over his stomach, he opened his jaws and howled, "For he's a jolly good fellow!"

Charlie's eyes shone with pleasure. No doubt about it, Ramsey could certainly perform when he wanted to. "That was great," Charlie admitted, "but what will I tell Dad? He might want to watch us practise."

Ramsey smiled broadly. He cocked his head and glanced sideways at Charlie. "Tell him to save up his money and catch the act at the fair!"

6

More Worries
for Charlie

During the next few days, Charlie tried to put the coming fair out of his mind. He was glad that his mother and father had not asked him about the act or if he was practising for it. Ramsey had decided what tricks he was going to perform and had given Charlie a short introduction speech to memorize. The dog told him to relax. "It's my act — you just present me," Ramsey insisted. Nevertheless, when he did think about the fair, Charlie got a funny feeling in his stomach and his throat felt tight. At those times he would look at Ramsey and remember the wonderful tricks that the dog could do. "After all," he tried to reassure himself, "nobody will be looking at *me*." But he could feel himself getting very hot and red just thinking about it.

Things went along smoothly, though, until Wednesday. Charlie was in the middle of sharing a bag of peanuts with Ramsey before dinner when a sharp rap on the door startled them. The dog sniffed the air. "It's your father, I think. The smell of these peanuts is almost enough to kill his scent." Ramsey brushed the crumbled shells under the bed with his paw. They were not supposed to be eating before dinner.

"Who is it?" Charlie called meekly.

"Dad," came the reply. "Thought I'd look in and see some of Ramsey's tricks, Son."

Charlie gulped and his stomach flopped over. He knew all too well that the fair was only a few days off. A picture of the stage and all the people floated before his eyes, and his knees felt like jelly. "Maybe Ramsey can do the act alone," he thought. "Maybe I can stand in the wings where no one will see me." But his thoughts were interrupted by the more immediate problem at hand. Would Ramsey perform for his father? He looked anxiously at the dog. Ramsey growled and shook his head, no. Charlie's mouth went dry.

"Well, Dad," he answered in a voice that he hardly recognized.

"Come on, Son. Open up."

Charlie brushed all the uneaten peanuts back into the bag and shoved them under the cushion on his chair. Then he went with lowered head to open the door.

"How about a preview?" his father asked. He walked across the room and sat down on the chair. *Crunch* — the peanuts cracked under his weight. He sprang up instantly.

"It's . . . it's nothing, Dad," Charlie hastened to reassure him. "That chair always creaks. Doesn't mean a thing, really."

His father looked sceptical. "I thought it had given way," he said, shaking his head and settling back gently into it.

"How about it, Son?" Mr. Rich looked expectant. "I'll bring on the act with applause." He clapped loudly, and a broad smile lighted his face.

Charlie shifted his weight and bit at his finger-nails. He looked at the dog, then cleared his throat and spoke in a coaxing tone. "Let's show Dad some of our act, Ramsey." The dog hid his face under the bed. Only the back half of him was visible, and it lay still. "Please, Ramsey," Charlie pleaded, "just a little trick." The dog slowly inched forward under the bed until he disappeared entirely.

"Well, I like that!" Charlie's father exploded.

"I don't," Charlie murmured. He lay down on the floor and peeked under the bed. The dog lay curled up in a ball, eyes closed, completely relaxed. Charlie poked his head under the bed and gave Ramsey a gentle shove with his hand. "Come on, just one little trick won't hurt," he urged.

The dog didn't even blink. Charlie heard a strange low sound. He scrambled farther under the bed and listened. There it was again, a low, steady *zzzzzzz*. Ramsey was snoring. Charlie was outraged. What a thing for that dog to do — pretend to fall asleep and leave him alone to face his father. What if Ramsey got to the fair and decided — Charlie pushed the thought from his mind. It was too awful to think about. But still, if he wouldn't cooperate and put on a little part of his act for just one person, then maybe . . .

"What's going on?" Mr. Rich asked.

He slid out from under the bed and looked up at his father. "Ramsey's been working very hard and he's exhausted," he said softly.

"How do you know that?" his father demanded.

"Because," Charlie whispered, "he fell asleep under the bed."

His father's jaw dropped. "Well, I'll be . . . That

must be a remarkable act to get him so tired out."

"Oh, it is," Charlie answered hopefully. He had the feeling that he was in the middle of a bad dream.

"Well Son, I hope you know what you're doing. Your act is one of the highlights of the fair. You don't want to disappoint anyone."

Charlie wished that his father hadn't said that the act was to be a highlight of the fair. The thought of it made his head light, and he had a peculiar feeling that it was floating above his body. And as if that weren't bad enough, he could picture the huge noisy crowds, even with his eyes open. They were all star-

ing at him, waiting for him to make a fool of himself so they could laugh even louder. Charlie's hands were clammy, and the back of his neck prickled. "I'll never be able to do it," he thought, "I just know I won't." Then he remembered that his father was waiting for an answer. He opened his mouth to say that he couldn't go through with the act, but nothing came out. He took a deep breath, cleared his throat, and in a peculiar voice found that he was answering, "No, sir."

His father smiled at him. "All right then," he said, "let the dog get some rest. Don't overwork him. But make sure that he learns the tricks." Mr. Rich turned and went out of the room.

Charlie waited until the sound of his footsteps faded, then he sighed deeply and closed the door. He was trembling as he moved across the room. Down onto the floor he went, scrambling under the bed. "Get up! I know you aren't sleeping. You didn't fool me one bit."

The dog opened one eye lazily and twitched his ears. He stretched in slow motion, and then raised his head abruptly. "What a pal you are, leaving me in the lurch," Charlie said accusingly. Ramsey's tail beat quickly back and forth, smacking the underside

of the mattress. "What have you got to say?" Charlie demanded, getting out from under the bed.

"We have a name for our act," the dog answered, following him. "Courtesy of your father."

Charlie calmed down. "What is it?" he asked.

"Remarkable. Charlie Rich presents the Remarkable Ramsey."

Charlie's face brightened for a moment, then clouded over. The name was nice enough, but it reminded him again of the awful fact that he had to speak to the crowd. He wanted to beg Ramsey to do the act without him, but he couldn't make himself admit his fear aloud. So instead he muttered, "It's fine, if we have an act."

"Have an act? Why, we'll have the most remarkable act they've ever seen," the dog bragged.

Charlie nodded slowly. He wished that the day of the fair would never come. Even if Ramsey put on the best act ever seen, Charlie was sure that he would never be able to get through it himself.

7

The Remarkable Ramsey

CHARLIE MOVED THROUGH THE CROWDS at the fair-grounds with Ramsey bounding at his side. The stalls were jammed with customers. Everyone seemed to be chewing on something. Hot dogs, potato chips, and candy floss marched by in twos and threes, and occasionally a whole battalion of ice-cream cones battered their way through the mobs. Charlie hoped his mother had ordered enough food. This year there seemed to be more people than ever at the fair.

Frank called to him as he and Mike elbowed by. "Hi, Charlie. Hear you have a dog act."

Charlie nodded unsmilingly and walked quickly on. He hoped he had a dog act. He looked down at Ramsey. The dog jogged along at his heels, scampering between legs and baby carriages. Charlie had a funny feeling in his stomach. He decided he was hungry, and pushed his way through the crowds to the refreshment stand. Putting his money on the counter, he ordered a hot dog and grape soda. Ramsey waited patiently for a piece of the hot dog, gulping it down quickly and busying himself licking a fallen blob of ice cream as he waited for Charlie to share the soda.

Frank and Mike joined them at the stand, ordering hamburgers and potato chips. "What's the act like?" Mike inquired.

Charlie smiled weakly. "You'll see," he answered aloud as he thought to himself, "I wish I knew." He stooped down quickly to share the grape soda with Ramsey.

"Will Charlie Rich and his dog act please report to the platform." The announcement blared out over the loudspeaker. The paper cup slipped out of Charlie's hands, spilling in the dirt and forming tiny purple rivers.

"Here we go. The Remarkable Ramsey," the dog

said. Charlie didn't move. His eyes stared vacantly ahead.

"Go on," Mike demanded. "They're calling your act." He and Frank pulled Charlie to his feet and gave him a shove in the direction of the platform. Charlie stumbled forward. Ramsey edged in front, taking the lead. The dog hummed softly off-key as he made his way through the crowd. Charlie tried to rehearse the commands for the act in his head as he stiffly followed the dog.

Ramsey shook himself thoroughly when he reached the platform, fluffing out his coat so that it was full and glistening. Then, with one great leap, he jumped onto the platform and surveyed the audience. His ears twitched to the noise of the crowd, and his tail stood at stiff attention. He trotted regally to the rear of the stage. Charlie stumbled woodenly up the platform steps.

"You Charlie Rich?" a tall, stout man in shirt sleeves asked, shifting his pipe between his teeth.

Charlie nodded. "That the dog?" The man jerked his thumb toward Ramsey. Charlie nodded again. "I'll announce your act. Wait a few minutes till everyone has a chance to get over here and settled down; then you can start. Don't let the noise throw you. A crowd like this hardly ever gives you its full attention."

Charlie smiled weakly and squinted out across the platform at the crowd.

"One, two, three, testing . . . testing." The microphone whistled loudly, and the announcer blew into it. "Ladies and gentlemen. Students and little ones.

Gather round for one of the biggest attractions of this year's fair. Our own Charlie Rich is going to give us a demonstration of dog tricks. Give him a big hand." The announcer motioned to Charlie to step forward while he lowered the mike for him.

"Please let him cooperate. Please, please, please," Charlie thought desperately, glancing back at Ramsey.

"Introduce your dog, then go into the act," the announcer whispered in Charlie's ear, and then leaped off the platform, leaving Charlie in charge of the microphone.

Ramsey had his back to the audience. His ears lay flat against his head. Charlie grabbed the microphone, ran his tongue over his lips, and looked out at the audience. "Ladies and gentlemen," he said in a small voice.

"Louder," a man's voice yelled.

"Louder — use the mike," someone else shouted.

Charlie looked square at the thing in front of him. He leaned forward until his mouth almost touched the microphone. "Ladies and gentlemen. Charlie Rich presents the Remarkable Ramsey." Not a sound greeted his announcement. Even the dog didn't

seem to respond. Charlie could hear his heart thumping like a drum. Then suddenly Ramsey turned sharply and bounded forward, his tail whipping the air furiously, his mouth spread in a wide grin.

Charlie swallowed hard. "The Remarkable Ramsey will perform some tricks for you," he said hopefully. He clutched the microphone and tried to recall the introduction the dog had coached him to say. He looked over at Ramsey for help. The dog's back was turned toward him and he was strangely quiet. "What's next?" Charlie whispered to him. There was no answer. Charlie put his hand over the microphone and repeated his request. Still there was no response. Charlie was seized with a sudden panic. Suppose Ramsey couldn't talk any more. Suppose he was just an ordinary dog. He stood biting his lip, and then he remembered what came next. "These are very difficult tricks for most dogs."

Suddenly Ramsey came alive. His tail whipped the air, and he pranced in front of the audience. "But I'm not most dogs," he said, twitching his ears and chuckling.

Charlie felt a little relieved and went on with his introduction. "But for your entertainment the Remarkable Ramsey will . . . will . . ."

"Demonstrate his unusual ability," the dog prompted.

"Will demonstrate his unusual ability," Charlie repeated, and backed away from the microphone.

The audience clapped politely. Ramsey marched back and forth, prancing slightly and nodding royally to the crowd. Charlie heaved a great sigh. "So far, so good," he thought, and he crossed his fingers on both hands and watched Ramsey for his cue. After the dog had allowed the audience to look him over thoroughly, he retired to the rear of the platform and inclined his head to Charlie. This was the cue for the first trick to be announced. Charlie cleared his throat and began. "Our first trick will be playing dead dog."

"Aw, my dog can do that easy," the clear shrill voice of a small boy rang out.

Charlie hesitated, then straightened his shoulders and snapped his fingers three times. Ramsey came bounding forward. Within a second he was front and center, head high, tail rigid at attention. Then, with deliberate care, he turned and began a stiff-legged stagger across the stage. Suddenly a shudder shook his body, his tail went limp, and he tumbled forward onto the stage. A hushed gasp rippled through the audience. He rolled over onto his back, his paws hanging limply in mid-air. Then his head snapped toward the crowd, eyes closed. His mouth fell open and a long red tongue oozed out.

"He's dead!" shrieked a little girl.

Charlie gasped and started forward. The sharp crack of clapping hands stopped him in his tracks. The crowd was clapping loudly. At the first sound of applause, Ramsey came alive. He was on his feet in a second, bowing low first to one side, then to the other.

"Three cheers for the trainer!" someone yelled.

Charlie followed the dog's lead; he bowed first to the left and then to the right. Then he held up his hands for silence, and a hush fell immediately. "We will now demonstrate catching and balancing this bracelet." Charlie's voice rang out loud and clear as he held up an old plastic bracelet his mother had donated to the act.

"My dog catches perfect," the small boy who had called out before bragged loudly.

"Yeah, like the way he can play dead as good as Ramsey!" an older boy shouted back.

Ramsey stepped forward. Charlie threw the bracelet into the air. With a flip of his head, the dog caught it on the end of his nose, twirled it around, and then tossed it high into the air. Up, up it soared. All heads snapped up to follow the bracelet. Then all eyes flicked down and remained fixed on the dog. Ramsey sidestepped quickly, letting the bracelet fall, like a hoop in a Hoop-la game, straight around his tail.

Charlie sucked in his breath. He could hardly believe his eyes. There wasn't a sound from the crowd. You could have heard a pin drop. And then with one great flip Ramsey tossed the bracelet off his tail, sail-

ing it into the air. Within seconds it landed, balanced perfectly on his back, standing on its end. Slowly Ramsey bowed, allowing the bracelet to roll gently down his back and over his head. Then he rose, the bracelet balanced delicately on the end of his nose.

"*Wow!*" a boy in the front row gasped, even as Charlie himself mouthed the word. The audience clapped and whistled. Charlie looked out across the stage. It seemed as if everyone at the fair had joined the audience. He had never seen such a huge crowd of smiling, cheering faces. Charlie stepped forward, grinning. He waved his hand in a sweeping gesture toward Ramsey. The dog was up on his hind legs, his front paws clasped together in a handshake like a prizefighter who has won a fight. Charlie laughed aloud, then turned and bowed gallantly in the dog's direction.

Then he called Ramsey to his side. "Let's really wow them," he whispered.

The dog's eyes shone, and his ears twitched excitedly.

"We'll do the fetch trick. I'll tell you who to fetch from. I'll pick boys who were at my party. Will you remember their names?"

Ramsey nodded vigorously.

"Ladies and gentlemen," Charlie's voice boomed into the microphone. "We have a super-duper mystifying trick for you now. We'll need a little help with this."

Hands flew up all over the audience: fat ones, thin ones, long ones, short ones, dirty ones, clean ones. And then the cry, "Pick me! Hey, Charlie — pick me!" rose up in a thundering roar.

Charlie grinned and held his hand up for silence. "Will the boys in my class please come up on the stage," he announced.

"Yipeeee!" The bloodcurdling yell resounded in the air as Charlie's classmates scrambled from their seats and trooped noisily to the stage. Charlie arranged them in a line across the middle of the platform, purposely calling each boy to his place by name. Ramsey sat wagging his tail, as he took in all the details.

Then Charlie addressed himself to the audience. "The Remarkable Ramsey will bring me what I ask for from the boys lined up here. The boys will not call the dog or help him in any way." Someone in the audience let out a long, low whistle. The boys on the stage shuffled and whispered to one another.

"Ready?" Charlie asked the boys. They nodded sceptically. "The Remarkable Ramsey will now demonstrate *fetch*." Charlie nodded to the dog. Ramsey got up, bowed to the audience, and trotted to the centre of the stage. "Ramsey will take the catapult out of Mike's shirt pocket and bring it to me. Fetch, Ramsey."

The dog winced at the word *fetch*, then chuckled as he approached the line. Confidently, he trotted past Frank, Tom, Jimmy, Arthur, and Don, and stopped directly in front of Mike. With a sudden leap he was in the air, snatching the catapult from Mike's pocket. A moment later he was prancing toward Charlie, the catapult dangling from his teeth. Charlie had to hold his ears, the cheering was

so loud. Mike was as white as chalk, and his mouth hung open. His hand still clutched his empty shirt pocket. "Again! Do it again!" the crowd shouted.

"Thank you," Charlie said into the microphone. "I will now ask the Remarkable Ramsey to fetch one shoe from each boy whose name I call." The smaller children in the audience began to giggle. The boys on stage leaned down to check the heels of their socks for holes. "Ready now?" Charlie looked toward the dog. He nodded and his tail beat the air. "Fetch a shoe from Frank."

Slowly Ramsey stood up, glanced down the line of boys, trotted a few paces, paused, and sat down. Turning his back to the audience, he allowed himself a satisfying scratch. Then he stood up, trotted the remaining way over to Frank, and nosed his left foot. The boy wiped his forehead dramatically and let out his breath. A lingering sigh passed through the audience. Frank leaned down and patted the dog's head. Then he slipped out of his shoe. Ramsey took the laces between his teeth.

"Fetch a shoe from Arthur."

Ramsey trotted down the line, while the crowd chanted, "Arthur. Find Arthur." Again they heaved a long sigh of relief when the dog tapped Arthur's right shoe with Frank's left one. "He did it again!" someone screamed. Arthur scratched his head and shrugged his shoulders. He removed his shoe while the crowd roared its approval.

"Fetch a shoe from Tom," Charlie demanded.

Ramsey made his way back down the line. A little girl's voice broke the hushed silence. "He'll find him. I *know* he will!" Ramsey stopped directly in front of Tom. He shifted the laces of the other two shoes in his mouth and picked up the third shoe.

"Bring them here," Charlie ordered. The shoes bounced and jiggled up and down and back and forth as Ramsey trotted over to Charlie and deposited them in front of him.

The entire audience, as well as the boys on the stage, cheered and clapped. Ramsey let the shoes fall with a thud. He sneezed loudly and snorted a few times as he pawed his nose. "No more shoes, *please*," he muttered.

Charlie laughed and turned to address his classmates. "Thank you for your cooperation. Ramsey will personally shake hands with each of you. But you'll have to collect your own shoes!"

Everyone began to laugh.

"Humph," the dog grumbled. "Where do you think up these ideas? Shake hands with *all* of them!"

"Three cheers for Charlie and Ramsey!" Frank shouted as he hopped over on one foot to join them and pick up his shoe.

The crowd responded with a rousing cheer, and only stopped their noise when Charlie took the microphone. "Thank you all very much," he began. "The Remarkable Ramsey and I have enjoyed bringing you our act."

"More! More!" a voice in the audience rang out.

Charlie grinned and glanced at Ramsey. The dog looked almost handsome, basking in all his glory. Charlie winked at him, and the dog winked back. "That's all, folks," Charlie told the audience. Then he turned and looked directly at Ramsey. The dog nodded. Charlie leaned close to the microphone and clutched it tightly. "Bye, folks. See you next year with another great act," he announced proudly.

His words had hardly died in the air when he realized what he had just said. He had said it all by himself. He had volunteered! His mouth dropped open in amazement. And then he noticed that his stomach felt fine and that he felt good all over. The thing he had most dreaded to do was over, and he was almost sorry. It had been exciting . . . it had been fun. He had enjoyed every minute of it . . . well, not every minute of it, he reminded himself. And suddenly he realized that he hadn't been as scared of the people as he had expected to be. In fact, he wasn't scared of people any more — not the way he used to be.

Charlie grinned. He bent down and buried his face in Ramsey's coat. "You know," he whispered to the dog, "I sure am lucky to have you."

Ramsey didn't say a word. He just stood there wagging his pointy tail.

If this book tends to
roam, box its ears and
send it home to

Karen Julie Hickman,
1, Arden Lodge RD,
Brooklands,
Manchester. 23.